How To Get
Fabulously
RICH

How To Get
Fabulously
RICH

THOMAS ROCKWELL
ILLUSTRATED BY TONY ROSS

ORCHARD

ORCHARD BOOKS
338 Euston Road,
London NW1 3BH
Orchard Books Australia
Hachette Children's Books
Level 17/207 Kent Street, Sydney, NSW 2000

First published in Great Britain in 1997
This edition published in 2014

Text © Thomas Rockwell 1990
Illustrations © Tony Ross 2014
The rights of Thomas Rockwell and Tony Ross to be identified
as the author and illustrator of this work have been asserted.

A CIP catalogue record for this book is available from the British Library.

ISBN 978 1 40832 428 8

2 4 6 8 10 9 7 5 3 1
Printed in Great Britain

Orchard Books is a division of Hachette Children's Books,
an Hachette UK company.
www.hachette.co.uk

CONTENTS

ASTROGOLY

"You think he's going to WIN?" yelled Alan.

"OH YEAH?" yelled Tom. "Well—" Something was pulling on the back of his pants. It was Billy; he didn't want Tom to argue? "Oh. Yeah." Tom began to shrug his shoulders around, as if he'd only yelled because of an itch or something. "Yeah. Well. You know." Why didn't Billy want him to argue? Billy wasn't even looking at him now.

"Know what?" said Alan. What was Tom doing, shrugging his shoulders around like Mum doing her yoga? It was scary when one of your friends suddenly started acting like your mother. "What are you doing?"

"Nothing," said Tom, turning his shrugging into touching his toes. "Can't someone exercise if he wants to? I had too much breakfast."

"Yeah. Well." Alan turned to Billy. "But do you really think you're going to win the lottery?"

"I don't know," said Billy, sitting down on a box. "Do you really think you're going to be Prime Minister?"

"What does that have to do with it?"

"Well you're studying history and maths and geography and science in school, aren't you, which is what you're supposed to do if you want to be Prime Minister?"

"Yeah, but that isn't like thinking you're going to win the lottery."

"Then why are you studying so hard?"

"He's not studying hard," said Tom, still touching his toes; maybe that was the way he could get into the

Guinness Book of Records: Tom Grout, most times touching his toes, 5,473,989. "He's got about four D's and three F's."

"We only get five marks, dumbhead," said Alan.

"Well, anyway," said Billy, standing up. "I gotta go. You coming. Tom? See you, Alan."

He pushed open the side door of the garage.

"Aren't you going to wait for Joe?" said Alan. "He's getting his mother's astrogoly book. So you can try to figure out your lucky number."

"Yeah," said Billy. "So I can win the lottery."

"Yeah."

"Like his mother has for the last nine hundred years, with her as-trol-o-gee book." He went out.

"You can't even pronounce the name of it," said Tom, running after Billy.

"At least I don't think I'm going to win the lottery with it!" Alan yelled after them. But then he realised it had been Joe who had suggested using the book to help Billy pick his numbers, now that he was paying Joe's older sister's boyfriend, Frankie Domino, to play the lottery for him. Of course, he wouldn't win—

"You want to bet he won't?" Tom's head appeared around the door. "Fifty pounds? Like on the worms?"

He disappeared. Alan could hear him and dumb Billy going off up the path, yukking.

ONE GUMDROP

"See, I don't think I'm going to win," said Billy, "How could I? In the last big drawing, you know, when the prize was fifty-two million pounds, the odds on someone winning were twelve million to one. That meant, see, like there were eleven million, nine hundred and ninety-nine thousand, nine hundred and ninety-nine other people besides you that bought a ticket—"

"I didn't buy a ticket," said Tom.

"No, I meant like if you had bought a ticket, there would have been eleven million, nine hundred and ninety-nine thousand, nine hundred and ninety-nine other people besides you who had. Of course, some of them would probably have bought more than one ticket, but that wouldn't make any difference really. See, my uncle explained it to me. He knows about computers and lasers and all that stuff because he's a doctor."

"What kind of a doctor?"

"A chiropractor."

"Chiropractors aren't doctors."

"That doesn't mean they don't know about computers and stuff! Come on!"

"Yeah. Well."

"So anyway, every one of those eleven million, nine hundred and ninety-nine thousand, nine hundred and ninety-nine other people who'd bought a ticket had the same chance of winning as you. It's like if someone went up in an airplane over Los Angeles, where there are like twelve million people, and he threw out one gumdrop. The chances that that gumdrop could land in your mouth, not someone else's, would be twelve million to one, see, so my uncle says anyone who buys a lottery ticket is like someone who walks around Los Angeles all day with his head back and his mouth open, waiting for a gumdrop to land in it."

"So then why are you buying the lottery ticket? You're even paying Frankie Domino to buy it for you."

"Because my mother – she's my uncle's sister – says—" Billy stopped. What his mother always said was "Faint heart ne'er won fair lady," and "You can do anything you put your mind to," "Never leave a stone unturned," "stick-to-it-iveness." But he couldn't tell Tom that, and besides, now that he thought about it, maybe she hadn't meant like the lottery. The trouble with parents was whatever they said, you had to translate it. It was gibberish, so you always had to get mothers to translate so everyone else could understand it. Billy stopped. What if it really was gibberish – parents really weren't saying anything – the mothers were just pretending so that everyone would think they were smart?

"So what does your mother say?" asked Tom. He'd stopped too.

"About what?" Billy had forgotten what he'd been talking about.

"About why you should buy a lottery ticket."

"My mother doesn't even know that I'm buying one."

"Yeah, but you said your uncle said it was stupid, but you were still doing it because of what your mother says."

"Oh. Yeah. Come on, I've got to get home." Billy pushed past Tom. "See, it isn't so much what she says; it's what she thinks."

"Boy," said Tom, "if you can tell what your mother thinks, you deserve to win the lottery."

"What do you mean?" Billy didn't really want to talk about why he was buying the lottery ticket.

"My mother's always saying stuff like 'Never tell a lie' and 'Speak softly but carry a big stick,' and then she's always yelling at people. Not that I care." Tom had just remembered what had

14

happened that morning before Billy had come to get him: Mum yelling at Daddy she didn't love him, she'd never loved him, why didn't he leave? But how could they have got married if they hadn't loved each other? And Suzy crying. That's what had started it: who was going to pick up Suzy at her piano lesson this afternoon.

They walked on silently till they got to the corner of Hooker Avenue.

"I'll see you."

"Yeah."

SWEET MELTED CHOCOLATE

Billy didn't really think he was going to win the lottery. But he didn't know; no one could know – even Albert Einstein or Sigmund Fruit couldn't know – he wasn't going to win. Crud. The phone would ring. They'd all be sitting around watching TV, Dad complaining about how they never did anything but watch TV and it was rotting their minds, Mum saying "Shh" because she was talking to Aunt Kim on the phone, Janie whining she couldn't ever hear because everyone was always talking. So then Dad's phone would ring, and Mum would pick it up, telling Aunt Kim to wait a minute. And then there'd be this long silence, so long that everyone would stop watching TV and turn to look at Mum, and her face would be like a Las Vegas neon sign, exploding with all different expressions, the hand that wasn't holding the telephone passionately mussing about in her own hair like on those cable channels you weren't supposed to watch...till finally Dad would yell, "Helen! What is it? Has the San Francisco earthquake returned riding on Godzilla's back?"

Billy banged through the back door of the shed to get the grain for the ducks.

Of course, it wouldn't be as bad as that. But anyway Mom would finally manage to gargle out through her foaming lips, "He won. He won." What? Who? Of course, he'd know. Geez, it'd be like – Billy stopped with the scoop in the grain – like all of a sudden he'd burst up out of the house, the walls collapsing. But it wouldn't hurt; he'd be like a giant, the whole town laid out below him. He'd lift the roof off Mrs. Picarski's house and, taking her between his thumb and forefinger, set her on the top of

her garage roof. And she'd be
shivering and begging him not
to hurt her, and he'd say in
this huge gruff voice. "I'm not
going to hurt you, hag Picarski,
I just wanted to inform you
that Billy Forrester won the lottery
and won't have his maths homework in on time
tomorrow, won't be in class tomorrow – won't be
in your class EVER!"

Billy filled the scoop, slammed
the lid back down on the can.

Of course, he knew if he
won the lottery he'd still have
to go to school – sometimes.
But like then so what if he got
an F in maths? He'd have to
buy four hundred computers to add
up all his money anyway. He'd buy a school and
only hire teachers like Miss Simons, who was nice
to people. She had long red hair and wore flowery
blouses.

Billy dumped the grain into the ducks' dish in their pen and then sat down in the grass, leaning back against the chicken wire of the pen; it sagged like a pillow.

He'd make Miss Simons principal, but Ms Falwell could come – and all the girls who were her pets, her brat pack, even Amy Miller – but only if she promised to stop acting like everything bad that had ever happened in the world – like war and starvation and persecutions – was men's fault, sticking pictures of famous women up all over her homeroom, making them do a whole month's chore on the Amazons, who probably had never even existed. And every time anyone like even by mistake pushed a girl in lunchline, she'd say, "Billy, no oppression." Or if you even half-pretended to fall off your chair when Joe's copy of the swimsuit issue of *Sports Illustrated* fell out of his desk, she'd spend the next six years talking about stereotypes and the terrifying oppression of media imagining. And she didn't have to be women's lib – not that Billy wasn't for women's lib because it really was like Mum said, women got paid less and everything. But Ms Falwell was pretty, so she didn't have to bother with all that – though she wasn't as pretty as Miss Simons – with her long red hair and flowery blouses. If you were walking behind her in a fire drill or out to recess, when she went from the shadow of the building into the sun, it was like – like her hair had suddenly burst into sweet delicious orange-juice fire. Except it was more like suddenly everything had turned into sweet melted chocolate inside you...like you'd just won the lottery...gold coins fluttering and tinkling softly down on you like a sun shower...

HELLISH GREED

Where was he? It was pitch dark. A smell of turd. Billy tried to sit up, but the hair on the back of his head was caught on something. He froze, so scared he was panting. Where was he? He couldn't remember. It was so dark it was like he was in a coffin, buried alive! He couldn't feel anything in front of him, around – his fingers touched something. He jerked them back; they'd almost been caught too! Like he was being swallowed by something. A hydramonster from outer space. Shh! He could hear something...

It sounded like – like ducks clucking quietly?

He realised he'd fallen asleep against the duck pen. He'd fed them and then sat down...

How long had he slept? He jerked his hair free of the chicken wire and scrambled up. There were no lights anywhere. Rip Van Winkle. Billy steadied himself by holding onto the chicken wire. He'd slept for ten thousand years; now he was the last person on earth. All around him lay the smouldering ruins of the last civilisation on earth. Everybody else had blasted off on space ships from the doomed planet.

He started to run and then stopped so quickly he fell down. If there were huge volcanic pits all around, he couldn't see...

Crawling, sweeping his hands over the ground ahead of him, he could feel it was grass like before, when earth was inhabited, when 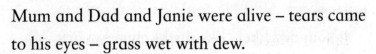 Mum and Dad and Janie were alive – tears came to his eyes – grass wet with dew.

A light!

Geez. He got sheepishly up, looking around to

make sure no one had seen him. He'd forgotten the garage was between him and the house, so of course he hadn't seen any lights. He brushed off his pants. Except he'd never seen a night this dark. It was like the stars had gone out. So maybe something really had happened. He listened. He could hear the traffic noises from the road. He looked up at the lighted windows of the kitchen. He still could have slept like in a coma so long that now strangers lived in the house. Green Martian glop people.

Come on. He ran tiptoe around the gravel driveway and got quietly up on the cellarway so he could look into the kitchen windows. Mum – she didn't even look any older – was talking on the telephone. So what else was new?

But Dad and Janie were just standing there, watching her – as if something really had happened.

Billy realised it was probably him, because he hadn't come home yet for dinner. The pots were steaming on the stove. He could rub dirt all over his face and limp in, one shoe off; he could even get red paint from the garage and smear some on his cheeks. Mum had hung up the phone and was talking to Dad. She was really upset.

Billy suddenly slid down the cellarway doors and ran up the backsteps and burst into the kitchen.

"Hi. Boy, you know what happened—"

"Billy!" His mother grabbed him, tilting up his head. She pushed back his hair. "Are you all right?"

"Sure. See, I fed the ducks and then I sat down to get a stone out of my shoe – and fell asleep!"

"Well," said his father. "That's a relief."

Janie was already climbing back onto the chair at the kitchen table where her colouring book was open, crayons scattered about.

"Billy," said his mother in an entirely different tone, "look me straight in the eye."

"I am."

Why did he always feel guilty even if he hadn't done anything?

THE KING OF SIAM

"My mother even says we can light a campfire," said Joe.

"Yeah, wow," said Alan. "And my mother's giving us hot dogs and marshmallows, and it's not going to rain. Camping out under the stars. Like explorers."

"Maybe I can get my father to lend us his camping dishes." said Tom. "It's only going to be behind Joe's house, so we probably wouldn't lose anything or leave it behind like before."

"I can't come," said Billy suddenly.

"You can't come?" said Joe. "What do you mean?" He nudged Alan. "Why not?"

"My parents have to go out, so I have to baby-sit my sister."

"We can get my sister to baby-sit, like we did last week when Alan's dad took us to the cinema."

"No, see, my parents—" Billy felt as if he were wading into a swamp. "My parents didn't like what she did."

"What she did? You didn't say anything before. They didn't say anything to her."

"Yeah, well, you know, it's your sister. I didn't want to hurt your feelings."

"Yeah. Well, so what did she do?"

Billy couldn't think of anything that was bad enough but not so bad that if Joe told Rena...

"My mother said not to tell you."

"Why not?"

"Because then if you told your mother, it would get into a grown-up thing, you know, your mother and father against mine." Billy began to feel like the swamp water was almost over his chin. "And, you know, then maybe someone might decide to sue, like for slander and lubble."

"You mean libel," said Tom.

"Oh, yeah, is it libel?" said Billy. "Really? How do you spell it? Boy, my mother says it's never too early to start learning words for college, it's—"

"No. Wait. Forget that," said Joe. "You mean my sister did something so awful your mother told you not to tell me?"

"To tell you the truth," said Billy, "she didn't even tell me. She didn't even want me to know. She didn't even trust her own son."

"Hey! Come on!" Joe shoved Billy and began to hop around like a boxer, jabbing the air with his fists, trying not to grin. "Anybody who's gonna say bad stuff about my sister is gonna have to answer to these fists! Boy. Come on, Alan, you know Rena. Ain't you gonna stand up for her too? Are you gonna be on my side, or am I gonna have to get my older brudder after the both of ya?"

"Oh. Yeah." Alan began hopping around awkwardly, jabbing with his fists.

Billy rubbed his mouth, looking at them, and then turned. "Yeah, big deal. You think you're so smart." He went off down the sidewalk.

Joe and Alan began to yell after him in smarmy voices:

"Lot-tery, lot-tery,
I'm gon' win the lot-tery"

Alan began to cavort like a long-legged stork, singing,

"Oh I'm the King of Siam, I am.

The whole world worships me.

I won the lot-ter-eee!"

Joe collapsed, laughing, onto the lawn, holding his stomach.

"He really thinks he's going to win."

"Are we still going to camp out?" asked Tom.

"Dumbo," said Joe, sitting up. "Don't you see he can't camp out because he has to be home when they announce the lottery winners tonight on TV? Oh geez."

DEY'LL ALL LIKE VOIMS
COME CRAWLIN'

"Hey, kid," said Frankie, letting the cigarette dangle dissolutely from his sullen lips. But it was a chocolate cigarette. "What's da number dis week? What's da good void?"

Joe's older sister, Linda, dissolved in laughter against him.

"You don't pay, I'll break ya legs!" screamed Frankie. "Get offa me, girl! Dat's da side my pistol's on." He pushed her roughly away. She collapsed over the fender of the car. "Dese streets are a jungle. Goniffs slouchin' here and dere, looking fer a angle. Where would you be without da money I give youse to buy dem fancy dresses and dat store-bought hair?"

Billy just waited, rubbing his mouth and looking at Frankie's knees so he wouldn't have to look at him but could say he was. It only made it worse if he tried to interrupt.

"OH!" cried Linda. "OH! So dat's da gratitude I get for beggin' da godfodder ta let you into da mob? Don't forget I'm gonna be his-a heir, da first female mafiacapitutti, Godmother Linda! Ha ha. Den who'll crawl ta kiss my littlest tootsie?" She tore off her sandal and threw it at Frankie, missing him and hitting Billy. "Tom Crusecontrol, Elvis Press-me-tohim! Dey'll all like voims come crawlin' to me."

Billy pretended to laugh. "Yeah. See, I have to go. My mother—" He pointed vaguely. He hated them so much. When he won, he'd hire real gangsters to beat them up.

"Go?" said Frankie. "Hey, doll, where's a no-good like him got to go?"

"Downhill to destruction and death," said Linda, suddenly serious. "So young and already so depravamolto."

Billy held out his two dollars and the piece of paper he'd written his numbers on. "Here's the stuff. Boy, I can certainly see why you two are going to be actors."

Frankie drew himself up and took the money delicately from Billy with the tips of two fingers. "Can you, my dear? You're so sweet. Eleanor Nobleworth, daughter of the Earl of Sus-sick, cousin-german to the Duke of Mess, heir to the Turdian throne, isn't this young man incroyable? So-oo, so-ah, so debonair."

"Thanks," said Billy. As he went off up the sidewalk, he heard them already beginning to argue about what number they were going to play. Linda was pretending to pout because he didn't want to play her birthday date again. He was fast-talking a historical system: start with the date of the Battle of Marathon and slowly work your way up through all the great battles of history, accumulating the karma of victory...

Billy wished he could play every number in the world. Then he'd have to win. Except Uncle Dick had explained that since numbers were infinite, you would have to have infinite money, which was more money than there was in Fort Knox, in the whole world. Billy didn't see how even a chiropractor could know how much money there was in the world. But he wished he could at least play more than just one number a week. He didn't believe in systems for picking numbers because it was all luck. The best thing to do was to pick the numbers without thinking.

If he went out behind the barn in the dusk – just when he thought he could still see things if he looked closer, but when he did, he couldn't tell what they were; they looked like six different things at once? And then he turned round and round and round till he was dizzy, almost a little sick to his stomach, and then he let his mind float, not thinking of anything but maybe a little clear cold water sloshing in whiteness...

And then, when numbers began drifting into his mind, he wrote them on the pad he was holding, though without letting himself really admit he was doing anything like writing, letting himself drift aimlessly around the lawn wherever his weight carried him, like a drunk person, almost falling down, his arms slack, head lolling, tongue hanging out...

So then the numbers were coming into his mind – if he could get it just right – just by chance, the same way they entered the mind of the machine at lottery headquarters that spit out the numbered Ping-Pong balls, from the same mysterious source, the dark heart of the universe

(Billy shivered), fate, the power that pumped luck into the farthest corners of the universe, saying when the teeniest flower or bird had to die – like in that poem Miss Simons liked to read out loud in class, "Oh wild west wind, pure sister of the spring, shall blow over the streaming earth and fill with living surge and blood and love both plain and hill."

FIVE MILLION DULLERS

Under the blankets and pillows, in the soft, almost inaudible flow of the murmurous love music from his Walkman, Billy had to keep pinching his lips to stay awake. Even the drops of sweat stinging his eyes didn't help. It was like nine thousand degrees. Why'd they announce the winners so late? Probably kids all over were getting sick, even dying, from not enough sleep and the heat and suffocation; soon the Communists would begin to take over... He started! Had he fallen asleep and missed it? He listened feverishly. His pyjamas were wet with sweat; he'd have to change. If Mum heard him, she'd want to know why. She couldn't really read his mind; tonight at supper he'd thought the worst things he could think – blood and naked women and people falling down cellar stairs – and she hadn't acted any different than she usually did. He'd even asked for a second scoop of ice cream and she'd given him one, even though he was supposed to be on a quarter diet for winter blubber like her.

No. He hadn't missed the announcement. It was still only nine fifty-five.

"Billy?"

Mum!

"Billy, wake up."

The covers were pulled
back. Mum and Dad.
They'd turned on
the lights.

"Billy, you've
won the lottery!"

"You're rich,"
said his mother,
clapping her hands.

"And we didn't even know you were sick," said his father.

"I won? I did?" Billy scrambled up and began to jump up and down on the bed, almost falling.

"Ten thousand pounds!" said his father. "They just called."

"Enough for so much," said his mother. "Treats now and college later."

Billy stopped jumping – partly because it was only ten thousand pounds. That would have seemed a lot of money before, but now, since he'd been studying money – like how much it would cost to buy a chocolate bar every day for the rest of his life if he lived to be forty-seven, which was ten years older than Dad and Mum were now, or how much Tottenham Hotspur would cost or the Tower of London – now ten thousand pounds didn't really seem like that much. Partly also because Mum had just said treats and college, which meant they weren't going to let him keep the money even though it was his, he'd won it.

And then he heard a voice as if his own feet were talking to him, or his conscience – as if someone like a murderer was hiding under the bed – a weird faraway tiny voice, so it seemed truer than a normal one: "– sharpening your pencils, folks? It's countdown to lottery time. Twenty, nineteen—"

"Billy!" said his mother. "You've been listening to that radio under the covers."

But she was smiling. But if...

"—twelve, eleven—"

"They called," said his father. "They said they always call the winners before the announcement. Everything's prerecorded, on tape delay."

"It isn't. I've read about it." Billy almost fell off the bed, fumbling the lottery booklet out of the drawer of his desk, leafing through it.

"Here. See. It's always live."

And then he realised what had happened.

"Mum, think: what did the voice sound like?"

"The voice?"

Billy ran to the window, pushed it up and leaned out, looking up and down the street. Two figures darted out of the bushes into the light of a streetlight.

"Oh, I'm the King of Tralee, Tralee.
There ain't no crumbs on me.
I've won the lot-ter-ee."

THE VENOMOUS
EGYPTIAN VIPER

"But Billy, two pounds a week? That's almost your whole allowance."

"You said I could spend it any way I wanted."

"But that's just wasting it."

"Lots of grown-ups play the lottery. But if you're not eighteen, you can't play it yourself, so you have to get someone to play for you." He had shown them his contract with Frankie. His father was reading it.

"But if you bought a book or something, even a toy, then at least you'd have something you could read or play with again."

"Mum, I'm not a kid any more. I don't just buy toys and sweets like Janie."

"And he's learning contract law," said his father. "This isn't a bad contract at all. I haven't counted, but I think it probably has enough 'wherefores' and 'whereats' to hold up in court."

"I copied some of it from your sample contracts," said Billy. "The ones you keep in the desk drawer downstairs for emergencies?"

"But he shouldn't be spending his time on something like that," said his mother. "He should be studying, doing his homework."

"Helen, you're like the people who complain about families on benefits buying television sets instead of something they really need. But people need entertainment. They have to be able to get away from things. People can't live like racehorses in the stretch all the time, straining flat out every second."

"But he only gets

three pounds a week. You certainly don't mean families on benefits should spend two-thirds of their income on entertainment."

"I have to go to the bathroom." Billy went off up the hall. Now they'd argue for half an hour over something that had nothing to do with anything. He wouldn't even be able to get to sleep. And then they'd finally get so mad at each other they'd take it out on him: No, you may never again play the lottery. Hitler and Mussolini have spoken. Billy stopped. He realised he hadn't heard the real winner. Of course, he knew he hadn't won. They'd probably take the radio downstairs with them.

"But look," said Billy's father, pointing his finger down at Billy, in bed with the covers tucked over his chin. (Mum was always saying it was impolite to point.)

"You can spend your allowance in whatever way you want. That's up to you. That's one of the reasons you're getting an allowance: so you can learn to make your own decisions. If you buy this you have to give up that."

"If you want to buy lottery tickets instead of something you could really enjoy again and again, like a book," interrupted his mother, "then that's your decision."

She acted like money wasn't as important as books; if he won the lottery, he'd be able to buy every book in the world.

"But," said his father. "And this is a big but." He grinned. "You're going to have to call off the dogs."

"It's not funny," said his mother, stooping to pick up his sweaty pyjamas.

"No, it really isn't," said his father.

"Especially since it's about the tenth time it's happened. First over the worm bet and then with the girls. What are those two boys' names, the ones who locked you in the closet in the barn and

45

just now pretended they were calling from the lottery?"

"Joe and Alan."

"OK. So you're going to have to settle it with Joe and Alan so there aren't any more midnight commotions. If anything like this happens again, no more lottery and I call their fathers."

His mother stooped and kissed him on the cheek. "Sweet dreams."

"Of millions," said his father.

"No. Of happiness," said his mother.

"Which is?" said his father as they went out, putting his hand on her shoulder.

"Something different for everyone."

The door clicked shut.

Billy didn't move. He liked the tightness of the covers over his chin when she tucked him in. Besides, they'd confiscated the radio. But they weren't going to make him stop playing. Little kids played with toys, Janie played house, Mum and Dad played tennis, he played the lottery. He stirred uncomfortably. So what was he worried about? He'd win, buy... He felt like something was holding him down even though he wanted to explode.

Suddenly he rolled over, wrenching the covers loose. Kicking and muggling himself all around, he tried to get the bed comfortable again. Then he lay still on his stomach, his face in the pillow. But it was still uncomfortable. He'd never win the lottery. It was stupid. His whole life was stupid. If he didn't lift his face out of the pillow, he'd suffocate. Then he wouldn't have to worry about being uncomfortable.
He saw his mother kneeling in the graveyard, weeping.

She'd dedicate her whole life to saving other children from smothering in their pillows, like a nun. He'd be famous. And then it'd turn out that even though he hadn't known it, of course, the last lottery ticket he'd bought, the one in his pants hanging on the chair by the window, had won.

The pillow was hurting his nose. He turned his head. But he still kept his arms straight down at his sides like someone in a coffin. Suppose tomorrow, when he was digging the new turn for the trail bike – Tom was coming after breakfast to help – his shovel hit something hollow. Thunk. And it turned out to be an old coffin. They'd get a pitchfork from the barn and lever up the coffin's lid...and inside there'd be this skeleton with gold doubloons in its eye sockets and this huge diamond clutched between its teeth! So someone would have to open the skeleton's jaws. But just as he was reaching towards the bony grey jaws, they'd hear hissing! Snakes had made a nest inside the skull. Venomous Egyptian vipers!

Planning an elaborate machine-contraption for extracting the doubloons and the diamond from the ancient snake-infested skull, Billy fell asleep.

ORGANISED GRIME

"So what's in it for us?" asked Joe.

"What do you mean?"

"Well," Joe put his hands behind his head and leaned back against the steps, crossing his legs. "What are you going to do for us if we agree to lay off?"

"If you don't, you're going to be in as much trouble as I am," said Billy. "My father'll call your fathers."

"Yeah, but they'd make you stop playing the lottery," said Alan.

There was a silence.

"You could promise to give them some of your winnings," said Tom He was sitting under a forsythia bush by the steps.

Joe rolled over and pretended to be puking off the side of the steps. "Oh, boy, that's such a – yuke glaw – good idea. Wow – yewg glolp – I can hardly wait to start spending the money."

"You should do it because we're friends," said Billy.

"Oh roop, yaw, agh." Alan, who was up on the porch, hung over the railing, waving his arms and retching.

"Alan Phelps," called his mother from inside the house, "what's going on out there?"

"Nothing."

His mother appeared in the door. "What were those awful sounds?"

"We were imitating birds, Mrs Phelps," said Joe, scrambling up. "For science class."

"Well. Just remember Alan's little sister is sleeping."

"You're committing a crime," said Billy. "Extraction. I've been reading about it."

"Extortion," said Tom.

"What do you mean?"

"It's extortion, not extraction. That's like dentists—"

"Come on. Anyway, it's like the Mafia goes to someone who owns a sweet shop and says somebody's going to beat you up and break your store windows if you don't pay us to protect you. That's what you're trying to do to me."

"So call the police," said Joe.

"Since you're illegally playing the lottery," said Alan.

Billy kicked the side of the steps.

"Alan!" called his mother from inside the house.

"I don't know why we always have to fight," said Tom. He was jabbing at the dirt under the bush with a stick. His mother and father just never stopped arguing. Last night his mother had yelled, "You married me, but you didn't buy

52

me. I'm not your unpaid housekeeper, I could get half of everything you own, half of this house, half—"

And then she'd looked up and seen Tom standing stock-still in the hall because he hadn't heard them when he'd come in the front door. So he'd felt like she'd meant they'd divide him in half too. "Every time something happens, we have to fight."

"I'm not fighting," said Joe.

Alan was leaning way over the railing to look at Tom, but he couldn't see him very well under the bush.

"What's the matter with you?"

"Nothing."

"My parents aren't going to make me stop playing the lottery because you're doing stuff to try to make me pay you," said Billy.

There was a silence. Billy got up. "Come on, Tom. Let's go get a soda. I'll pay."

"Good luck," said Joe. "Don't say we didn't warn you."

Alan waited until Billy and Tom had crossed the street. Then he said, "What are you going to do? He's right. His parents aren't going to be mad at him because it won't be his fault."

"Do I look worried?" said Joe.

Alan looked at him.

"No!" he yelled suddenly. "Oh no! You're not worried! Because you're going to think up this big PLAN! You're so SMART! Just like you were with the worm bet, just like you were with Amy Miller and your sister! Oh no, you're not worried!"

He ran after Billy and Tom. "Hey, wait."

After a while Joe stood up. So what? Alan Dumkoff. All he ever did was complain; he never helped. He'd made the stupid worm bet; Joe had even told him it was stupid. Screw them. He had better things to do. If he'd had anything better to do, he wouldn't even be here now. He started down the walk and then turned and came back, went up on the porch, and knocked on the door. Alan's oldest sister came down the hall wiping her hands on a dish towel.

"Yes?"

"Alan said to tell his mother he won't be home for dinner because he's gone with Billy to the City."

HOMESICK

"I only have enough for two sodas," said Billy, showing his money to Alan.

"He can have mine," said Tom.

They both turned to look at him.

"Why don't you want one? "

"I don't know," Tom shrugged. "I just don't feel like it."

After Billy had got the sodas, they sat down on the kerb in front of the shop.

"You want a drink?" Alan held out his can to Tom.

"Nah."

"What's the matter?" asked Billy.

"Nothing."

"There must be something the matter if you don't want a soda."

Tom shrugged.

"Is your mother sick?"

Tom shook his head.

"Here," said Billy, holding his soda out to him. "Take a drink."

"No! I don't want any! I told you."

"You don't have to get mad."

"I'm not."

"You're not happy."

"Would you be? Just leave me alone."

"Would I be if what?"

Tom didn't say anything.

"Yeah, what?" said Alan.

"I think my parents are getting a divorce."

"How do you know?" said Billy. He knew what divorces were, but he didn't know much about them.

Tom shrugged.

"My father used to joke about it," said Alan. "So my mother finally said if he didn't stop, she'd eat in the kitchen, so he said, well, he could talk about anything he wanted at his own dinner table. But he stopped joking about it as much."

"What was the date of their wedding?" said Billy suddenly to Tom.

"I don't know."

"Geez," said Alan. "He says his parents are getting a divorce, and all you're thinking about is the lottery?"

"No. I just happened to think of that too."

They watched a woman pulling a little girl along the sidewalk across the street. The little girl was pointing back at a cat sitting on a stoop, washing.

"You could at least let him choose the numbers this week," said Alan. "To take his mind off it. And then if you won, you could give him some of the money. That's what his parents are probably upset about. My parents are always arguing about what my grandmother costs."

"Sure." Billy shrugged. "He can help. I just have to know by Thursday."

ELBOW PUNCHES

"Mum," said Tom. "What day did you get married?"

"Gloomy Thursday," said his mother. She shut the freezer, her mouth full of ice cream, and threw the spoon in the sink.

"No, really," said Tom. "Why are you going off your diet?"

"I'm not going off my diet. I'm allowed three Treat Moments a week."

"That big?" said Tom. "That was more like a treat bathtub. Or a treat weekend."

"Or a whop," said his mother, pulling down the visor of his cap, "which is what you'll get if that homework isn't finished by the time I get back."

She went out. Tom heard the car start. Tom's older sister, Betsy, came into the kitchen holding up her hands, her fingers spread, so her nail polish would dry.

"Do you know what day Mum and Dad got married?" asked Tom.

"I'll never get married," said his sister, sitting down across from him.

Tom realised she couldn't do anything to him because of the nail polish. "You could save up for plastic surgery."

She jumped up, knocking over her chair. Tom started to run, but she'd already darted around the table and tripped him with her foot. She plopped down on his back and began to belabour his head and shoulders with her elbows.

"Stop it! You're hurting me! I'll tell Mum!"

There was a knock on the back door.

Dave Anderson, her boyfriend, was peering in through the curtains – though probably he couldn't see them behind the table.

"If you say anything..." she hissed in Tom's ear, and then stood up. "Hi Dave. Come on in."

She ground her bare heel into Tom's back, hissing out of the corner of her mouth, "Don't you say anything."

Dave came in.

"I was just helping Tom pick up his papers," Betsy said. "He's so clumsy. You shouldn't see me like this, doing my nails, in my bare feet."

"Practising walking on people for when you're married," said Tom, getting up.

"Practising walking on eggs," said Dave, "for when you're married."

"She just said she's never getting married," said Tom, keeping the table between him and his sister.

She tossed her head, her eyes helpless, still holding her hands out.

"She's getting married this June," said Dave.

"What day?" said Tom. The day that Betsy got married would be luckier than Mum and Dad's anniversary. Besides, Mum and Dad had got married so long ago, before he'd  been born, that it almost seemed like it didn't matter any more, like the Battle of Hastings.

"Either the tenth or the seventeenth," said Dave, grinning. "She hasn't decided yet."

"Oh, Dave!" She grabbed him, hugging him, forgetting about her nail polish. Tom made a face. It was disgusting. They were really kissing like in the movies; their lips and noses, their whole

heads, were churning around like they were in this horrible agony. Tom started to gather up his homework.

"Oh, Dave!" Betsy pulled her head back, radiant. Tom noticed there were smears of red nail polish like blood all over Dave's face, like he'd been clawed. But Betsy did look pretty.

Tom edged further out of the dining room window so that the sill was against his thighs, as if he were the figurehead of a ship. He wondered what the world record for hanging out of windows was. Of course, it depended on how you measured it – like how high up the window was or if the wind was blowing. At the Shard, he'd kept a little hunched over the whole time, with his jacket zipped so the wind couldn't get into it and balloon him off over London – first like Superman, then like a rock when you throw it so high you think it's never going to stop going up, but it always does. He glanced down at the ground and almost lost his balance, grabbing the window frame, slithering, scrabbling back in. It was so much further down than he'd thought!

But when he looked over the windowsill from inside, the lawn didn't look far down. Except he'd heard of lots of people falling out of first-storey windows and fracturing their skulls.

Finally, he went out to the garage and got the stepladder and, setting it up against the window – first looking round to make sure no one was watching – he managed to squirm feet-first into the window and then, hanging onto the ladder so tight his hands hurt, he lowered himself till his knees were caught over the sill. Then he walked his hands down the ladder slowly…let go… pushed it away. It fell over.

Now how could he get back down?

He tried to twist round so he could see how high off the ground he was and twisted too far! He fell crookedly into a heap, banging his head against the foundation.

But he hadn't really hurt himself.

Hanging again by his knees, Tom triumphantly shut his eyes and imagined he was dangling by one foot caught in some wires hanging from the top of the Shard.

"Woooo woooo" – he made wind sounds – "beep beep," faint street noises. Then he whispered, "His mind emptied, cleansed, scoured by the danger – a single slip would send him flying to eternity…eternity…eternity…" He focused on numbers, lowering himself slowly, magically, to the street in a hypnotic basket made of numbers… thousands, millions, trillions of magic numbers… 41 72 37 88 99 102 16 61 23 5 19.

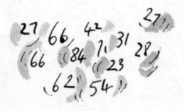

A Grey Steel Apple

Billy sighed and sat down on his bed. His cigar box of old lottery stubs lay open on his desk. He'd only been playing seven weeks. He hadn't realised he'd been playing that long already. Fourteen pounds. He looked at the slip of paper in his hand: 72 45 84 95 21 78 17 55 62 90 39. The numbers didn't seem right. He read them again. If he could just see behind or around the numbers to what they were going to become: huge glorious neon boastful winning numbers or just stupid little nothing pea-brain defeated numbers. But you had to believe in your numbers. If you didn't, the energy wouldn't flow from you through them into the ping-pong balls at lottery headquarters.

Of course, that was bunk. It was all luck. My lucky number: 72 45 84 95 21 78 17 55 62 90 39. Except maybe you really could figure it out scientifically. Everybody used to believe the world was flat. So if you got a pad of paper and your calculator... He got a pad and his calculator out of his desk drawer, sat down, and moved the lamp closer. So if he worked as hard as he could until he got it right – even if it took him forty days and forty nights...

OK. He went downstairs and sharpened all his pencils.

OK. First number: 72. It seemed like a good number. Six 12's are 72. That was magical. You were suddenly transported, like on a magic carpet, all the way from 6 to 72, without doing anything, without knowing how you'd done it – 6 x 12, abracadabra, and you were in the strange faraway land of 72. You'd got through the complicated hen-scratch teens – 11, 12, 13, 14 – the strange but still homey twenties, the uncomfortable thirties, the forties, fordable only because 2 + 2 = 4 was the nicest, surest thing, like stabbing soft butter with a sharp knife. And then came 50, like a pyramid, halfway between 0 and 100. But then on the cold northern slope of it lay the ravines of the fifties – nothing went into 5 evenly – though the path started up smoothly again at 60. But then everything really fell to pieces in the seventies, 7 was even worse than 5. It wasn't even half of 10; 7 was nowhere.

Counting backward was better. Everything kept getting simpler and simpler as you went slowly carefully down the long staircase toward home. Of course, you couldn't take

the exciting up escalator of multiplication if you were counting backwards: 88 87 86 85 84...

What about a humongous number like 96739976318839426719?

Billy's mind swam. He took a deep breath. 72. Should he try to get the feel of, glom, the whole number at once, in one breath? Or first the 7, then the 2? It'd be better if he had all the numbers written on separate pieces of paper. 1 was the beginning: out of the bottomless hole of 0 bounded 1. And then there was 2. So 2 was exciting, though you could never be sure where the other 1 had come from. Like Adam and Eve? But usually if there was a 2 around, you felt you could do something – at least you had a chance – you didn't get that awful empty feeling as if the teacher was asking you to eat a grey steel apple.

So OK. 72 was all right, perfect.

Now, da dahhh! 45.

Billy tried to stare into the depths of 45. Or if he could suddenly look away and then back so fast his eyes would ricochet off 45 into the land where all the secrets lie, the nth dimension, where the lakes were yellow custard and when you wanted to sleep, you just lay down on the warm air and floated...

Zero was all right as long as it was attached to something. Or you could roll it along the page with your pencil like a hoop. But 9 was really even worse than 7. But you could always rush past 9 to get to the promised land, 10. Then you could just sit down and rest or leap along the tens like stepping stones, 10, 20, 30, 40, 50, 100, 1000, 10,000, 10,000,000, 100,000,000, heaven.

Billy realised he was like a kindergartener heaping up mud, not even making mud pies, just glopping around with the numbers until they seemed to fit together in some way, even a weird

one. It was like gluing one
block on top of another
at the points of two
corners – like that
sculpture he'd seen
at the museum with
Mum – which was
scary and interesting,
but it wasn't real. Gluing
was cheating.

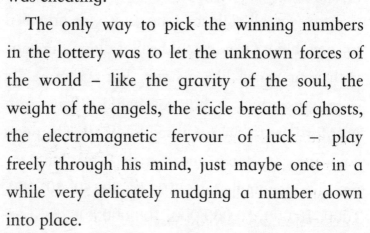

The only way to pick the winning numbers in the lottery was to let the unknown forces of the world – like the gravity of the soul, the weight of the angels, the icicle breath of ghosts, the electromagnetic fervour of luck – play freely through his mind, just maybe once in a while very delicately nudging a number down into place.

But it was discouraging. It took so long probably to work everything into just the right alignments. What good would it do to win the lottery when you were so old you could hardly walk? Like Mum always talked about how she'd been on the field hockey team and the star centre on the girls' basketball team, but he couldn't even look at her if she ran now; it was sort of like her arms and legs all flew out every which way like a toy rope horse. And after she'd gone not even to the mailbox, she'd stop with her hand on her – um – throat, panting, her face all blotchy red. And then she'd lift her hair and wave air under it because she hated to sweat under her fringe.

Now he'd even forgotten where he was, what he was doing.

Lost in the endless forests of numbers. Nowhere.

The trouble with playing the lottery was you could never be sure you were going to win because you kept losing. And how did anyone really know the winners they showed on TV weren't fake, just actors the lottery commission hired. The lottery commission. "The commission" was the name of the criminals' organisation in Batman or some other comic book. Nobody ever really won the lottery. The commission just pretended there were winners and used ALL the money for education. They had a secret contest in a locked resort in the Cotswolds, and the meanest headteachers, and the teachers who just like clubbed their students over their heads with homework, buried them alive under it, they won huge cash awards. So like Mrs Picarski had this secret underground castle like Hitler under her house with college students who were on probation slaving to figure out impossible essay questions, lashed on by bald computeresses.

Billy puffed. Geez, now he was all hot and sweaty. He

went down the hall to get a drink of water. At least it showed how hard he was working. As he passed Janie's room, he heard her counting, "Thirty-one, forty-nun, diddly bop burp. So the first number's oop. Janie dear, you're being such a good girl. Mithmatic's so tiring."

Billy dashed back to his room, snatched up pencil and pad, ran back.

"—mynie mo, catch an ostrich by the toe. If he hollers, let me GO! So the second number's go. One flower on the wallpaper, two flowers on the wallpaper, ninety, four hunnerd, two thousand, a zillion flowers all over the walls. So the third number's wah."

She sang quietly to herself for a while. Billy wanted to yell at her, Go on! Go on! But he knew that would ruin it. Finally, her humming began to change to serious buzzing. She was moving around the room.

"Frying, frying. Frying so high my head hits the sky!" A pause. "So the next number's bump. And then all fall down. So the next number's" –

she giggled – "heinie."

Their mother called from downstairs, "Billy, Janie. Dinner."

Billy frantically counted the letters of the words he'd written. Only nineteen. He needed three more. But Janie was talking to her doll, Janice, now getting her ready for dinner. It was like that nursery rhyme, "for want of a nail the kingdom was lost." He'd never realised nursery rhymes were true.

"—comb your hair ten hunnerd times," said Janie. "There. So now we're ready."

Billy saw the doorknob begin to turn. It was going to be too late!

Janie came out with her back to him, pulling the door shut, and then turned and saw him and looked a little startled.

"Boo?" she said.

"No," he said. "No boo. I was going to the bathroom."

She went round him. "So the last number," she said to Janice as they started down the stairs, "the last number, dear sweet Janice, is boo."

Billy ran back to his room. Of course, now he had to translate the letters into numbers.

Wait. He'd read about this code once. Each letter was given the number of its place in the alphabet.

"Billy. Phone for you," called his mother. "And dinner's ready."

It was Tom. "I got my numbers. Wait'll I tell you how I got them."

"My mother's calling me for dinner."

"Well, have you got a pencil? We're going away, so I have to give them to you now."

"OK. Go on." Billy wrote down the numbers, not that he was going to use them. You could tell Tom wasn't ever going to win the lottery just by looking at him. Except maybe if you counted the little brown moles in his face...

But there were more than 22 numbers because, of course, after I, the ninth letter of the alphabet, the numbers were all double. Billy counted. There were 33 numbers, 16½ pairs. Geez. Why was everything so hard? Wait. That was 11 pairs, which is what he needed, and 5½ other pairs. Exactly half: 5½ and 5½ made 11. So that had to be a sign that if he could find the right combination of the three sets of 5½ pairs... Of course they weren't going to make it easy. The hero always had to do something incredibly impossible like drink a lake or see through a mountain. Try the first 11 pairs first, then next week try – but it was probably only good for this week; he had to get it right the first time. If he wrote the pairs on little bits of paper? And then got Janie to pick 11 out of a hat!

Big Foot

Billy threw back the covers and stood up on his bed. He looked wildly around. Then he threw himself back down on the bed and scrabbled the covers into a heap over his head. A mistake!

He might have heard wrong because at the end he'd been so excited. The voice on the radio said:

"OK, folks, now here's the second repetition. We always repeat it because—"

Write it down! Billy fell off the bed, dragging open the drawer of the table beside his bed, turning up the radio full-blast. A pencil! He had a pencil but no paper!

"OK now, folks, the winning numbers for

Saturday, 15th April..."

Billy wrote on the wallpaper: 59 16 71 23 18 23 95 – his pencil broke. He had to gouge the last numbers into the wallpaper. It didn't matter. Tomorrow he'd paint them six feet high in red all round the outside of the house! 14 31 22 68. He switched on the light on his bedside table and reached tremblingly into the pocket of his pyjama shirt – it wasn't there! He rummaged frantically through the mess of sheets, blankets. He couldn't have lost the winning ticket. He imagined a corner of it sticking out of the mud and debris of a gutter somewhere down the street. He found it on the floor beside the bed, compared it to the numbers on the wall three times, and then SCREAMED! He threw up the window and screamed out, "I WON!" then began throwing stuff up in the air – pillows, clothes. He jumped up on the bed, off the bed – how much had he won? He grabbed the radio. They were already just playing music. Maybe it was still on TV. He ran out into the hall, colliding with his mother.

"Billy, what—"

He dashed past her, down the stairs, almost falling.

"You won?" called his father.

Janie wailed from her room, "Mummy, Mummy, I hear a robber or maybe it's BIG FOOT!"

She began to cry.

THE CALM BEFORE
THE STORM

"I'll sleep," said Billy as his mother tucked him in. "Boy, will I sleep! This is the greatest night of my life!" He sat back up. "Somebody might try to steal the ticket! While we're sleeping!"

"They don't give out the names and addresses of winners," said his father. "You have to go with your ticket to claim your winnings."

"Oh. Wow." Billy flopped back, pulling the covers over his head.

"But do try to get some sleep," said his mother. "My lottery winner."

She kissed the top of his head. They went out.

Under the covers Billy tried to understand what £410,000 really was. A heap of ten-pound

notes as big as a pillow. He hugged
his pillow, kissed it, snuggled
his face down into it. He
rolled over and gazed
up at the ceiling.
The lights of a car
swelled weirdly across
the ceiling, vanished –
it was partly because they
reflected off the porch roof. He
multiplied against the light wave of another
car, writing in the air with his finger: forty-one
million pennies, 41,000,000. He'd go over to
Tom's house tomorrow, and Alan and Joe would
be there, and at first they wouldn't believe him,
and then, wow, they'd all dance around yelling
and screaming and all the neighbours would
come out and want to shake his hand and
congratulate him.

And he'd go on TV, probably with Mom and
Dad and Janie standing behind him, all dressed
up, and they'd ask him what he was going to do

with the money. And he'd yell, SPEND IT! No, he'd say, Well, college. And then Mom would lean forward and say, After he's bought himself some presents – like a Harley-Davidson 7000 hog, loaded, and a speedboat to sheeeeeee, shooooooo, zup zup round the lake, bouncing over his own wake. And everybody'd scream and try to flag him down because his humongous wake was flooding all the docks and carrying toys and picnic baskets and even little babies and old ladies out into the lake.

No, not really. Except maybe he really would enter one of those professional speedboat races, bent over the wheel in the bubble cockpit, coolly busy adjusting dials, levers, glancing at the radar, fired up because in the back of his mind he knows one slip-up, just grazing a floating log, can mean instant DISINTEGRATION! There was that boat last year on TV – one moment it'd been there, charging through the water, and the next it had vanished, a few tiny bits and pieces floating in the air and then nothing, not even a

dimple on the water. And
then he'd climb out of
the boat, wiping the
blood and grease
from his face, and
the beautiful Miss
Powerboat Tender (Miss
Simons) would put a medal

round his neck and kiss him. And then he'd
stand up on the boat and beat his chest
like Tarzan and give the call of the gorillas
like the wild west wind, and the crowd would
"suddenly grow grey with fear, and tremble and
recoil themselves".

Of course, not really. But probably
they'd have a parade down the High Street
for him, and if he was late for school, well, Mr
Meachem would talk to him, but it would be
like man-to-man now that he'd won the lottery:
Of course, rules don't apply to you, Billy, in the
same way, but we have to set a good example
for children. Yes, yes, he understood. Then he

and Mr Meachem would both light up big cigars and maybe have a dish or two of ice cream sent over from the cafeteria.

No, not really. But it really would be as if he was like nineteen feet tall. He'd stroll down the street, flipping pennies to the noisy crowd of little kids fawning after him, and when he got to the corner, the chief of police would stop traffic so he could cross. And then the bank president would come running out to ask him if he wanted any money that morning? So he'd say, yes, about a wheelbarrow full.

No, not really. But...

THE GOLDEN YOLK

Billy went out on the front steps, licking off his mouth and cheeks the last of the maple syrup and blueberry pancakes Mum had made to celebrate. He stuck his thumbs in his belt and looked round at the neighbourhood. It was like everything looked worse and everything looked better all at once. He felt like the perfect golden yolk of a fried egg. If you pricked him, he'd run all over everything. He could buy any of the houses he saw. He could buy a house! Not that he wanted to. He took a deep breath, heaving out his chest.

He was acting like a jerk. He took his thumbs out of his belt. Geez. Come on. He tried his hands in his side pockets, took them out. The trouble was, he didn't know what to do with his hands now; if he just let them hang, it didn't feel right, but putting his thumbs in his belt like he was the president of the United States felt stupid. He tried putting them in his back pockets, putting one in his shirt like Napoleon. Clasping them on top of his head felt best. But he couldn't walk down the street like that, like a prisoner of war. And it wasn't just his hands. He didn't feel comfortable no matter how he stood – one foot forward, feet apart this much, this much... He lost his balance and almost fell over. Even his clothes didn't feel comfortable – like he could feel them sort of not fitting quite right all over, pulling here, too loose there. And now he was starting to itch – the back of his neck, his elbow, behind his knees, down inside his running shoes. Geez, if this was what winning the lottery was like... He sat down in one of the rockers. He'd heard rich people were unhappy, but he'd never believed it. Well, if their parents died – Dad and

Mum weren't going to die! Now he was getting DEPRESSED!? It was crazy! He'd just won the lottery! He began to rock faster and faster,  faster and faster, faster and faster! And then, on a down rock, he took off, leaping over the porch steps to hit the ground galloping, waving his arms, yelling, running along the pavement...till he had to slow down because he was panting so hard he couldn't think of anything but trying to catch his breath.

And after that he was all right – just if he felt the weirdness coming over him again, he'd wave his arms around and skip or run leaping along or shadowbox, sliding his feet as if he were skating. So it took him a lot longer than usual to get to Tom's house, and he fell down twice and tore the knee of his pants and scraped his elbow. Once a little girl ran into her house yelling, "Mummy, Mummy, I think there's a real leprechaun coming down the street!" and an old man waved his cane at him and called him a drug addict.

UNGRASPABLE ENORMITIES

But when he got to the corner of Tom's street, he stopped and wiped the sweat off his forehead and combed his hair with his fingers and walked as if nothing had happened, trying to whistle. But he couldn't keep his lips wet; even when they were wet, they wouldn't work right; he kept tweeting, he was so excited, rehearsing how he was going to say it. "Oh yeah, I'm all right, nothing much doing, I won the lottery." or, "Down on your knees, dogslaves, or DIE!" or, "No, Mrs Grout, I didn't come to see Tom. I came to buy your house," or, "Please, Mister Alan and Mister Tom, would you please come KISS MY SMELLY FEET!" or, "Well, yes, old Grandfather Grout, I used to be your grandson Tom's friend, but now I'm only thinking of employing him as my chauffeur."

Tom and Alan (unfortunately, Joe wasn't there) were playing boccie, Italian bowls, with Tom's grandfather in the backyard. Tom's grandfather was Italian and had taught them all how to play. But before Billy had a chance to say anything, Alan said, "What's the matter with you? You look like you just got run over by a truck."

"Your shirt's on backwards," said Tom.

"And your fly's unzipped."

"Your shoe's undone."

"You got blood on your cheek."

Billy just looked at them. Then he said slowly, "Four hundred and ten thousand."

"What?"

"Four hundred and ten thousand."

"Tom, your-a play," said his grandfather.

"What do you—"

"You mean we won?" said Tom.

Billy nodded his head. "Yep. I won the lottery."

"Nah," said Alan. "He's faking it, Tom."

Billy shrugged "Call my father."

Tom suddenly turned and ran toward the house, yelling, "Mum, we won the lottery! Billy and me won the lottery! Mum!" He disappeared up the steps into the kitchen.

"I should get something too," said Alan suddenly. "It was my idea for Tom to pick the numbers. If it hadn't been for me, you wouldn't have won."

Billy just looked at him. It was like he could see every hair in his nostrils, all the tiny specks and pores around them, and then his whole nose was growing, swelling, like a nose in a funhouse mirror. His whole face became huge and narrow and long, with this huge curved nose growing, thrusting toward Billy like it was going to eat him up… A screen door slammed.

Mrs Grout was rushing like an enormous soft balloon down the steps, across the lawn.

She hugged Billy to her, almost suffocating him like a huge disgusting perfumed pillow. Then she pushed him back out to arm's length. "You and Tom won!" She hugged him in, dropped him, turned to grab Alan. When he emerged, he was in the midst of saying, "make them give me—"

"What's a matta you, Nelly?" said Tom's grandfather. "What's a matta everyone?"

"Papa, Tom won the lottery!"

Tom's father grabbed Billy's hand. "Let me congratulate one of the winners!"

"Give me some! Please!" One of Tom's sisters grabbed Billy's other hand. "Please. Just a little. Oh, I can't believe it."

"If anyone never deserved to win—" said

someone. People were running across the lawn. Both Tom and Billy were surrounded. Tom's grandfather was picking up the boccie balls from under people's feet, grumbling.

But suddenly Billy, manhandled like a rag doll a pack of dogs are playing with, unable to say anything at all – suddenly Billy wrenched free of someone, the next, ran, fell down, gravel biting his knees, hands, almost beginning to cry, scrambling up, running...

A Tangle of Lies,
Memory and Money

"But did you tell him you'd give him part of it if you won?"

"But I didn't use his numbers," said Billy.

"I know," said his father. "But just answer me: did you tell him you'd give him part of it if you won?"

"I don't know. Alan might have."

"It doesn't matter what Alan said. Did you say it? Try to remember."

"You were sitting on the steps of Alan's house," prompted his mother.

"I don't know. I told you. It was like we were talking— No! It was when we were drinking sodas, in front of the corner shop." He hesitated. "But I still can't remember. It was like we were just talking."

"John, I don't see why you're worried if—"

"It's a verbal contract."

"But if they're minors and can't make contracts—"

His father sighed and stood up, stretching. "I don't know. I'll have to call Larry Enright in the morning.  My God." He sat back down at the kitchen table, wrote something on his yellow legal pad, turned back the page and, writing "The Numbers" at the top of the new page, turned to Billy. "OK, now let's focus on the numbers."

"You mean if he said he'd give some of it to Tom," said Billy's mother, "then he's going to have to?"

"Maybe. I don't know."

"But if that's what you think they're going to say, isn't that what we should be concentrating on?"

His father looked at his mother then sighed and got up and went over and leaned with both arms against the counter, looking out at the backyard. The refrigerator thunked on.

"Helen, look. If we don't go at this systematically, if we just get upset and—"

"I'm not upset."

"—we'll never get anywhere. It's just we've got to think of every little thing. This is a lot of money. You don't know what happens to people when there's this much money involved. They do crazy things. What Billy said to Tom is important, but now—" He came back around the table. "Now let's concentrate on the numbers."

"Because that's the other part of it, Billy," said his mother. "First, if you said you'd give him part of what you won and second if you used his numbers."

"I didn't. I told you." He looked down at his hands, though he didn't see them, didn't even feel how hard he was rubbing one finger, because he'd suddenly realised that in a way he'd used numbers he'd got from Janie. So he'd have to give her part of his money too?

"Why didn't you use his numbers?"

If they'd just stop bothering him so he could think…"I told you. I had better ones."

"Did you write his down?"

"I don't remember."

"It's important. If you'd written it down, what would you have written it on?"

The phone rang. Billy's mother answered. A moment later she put her finger to her lips, raising her eyebrows at Billy and his father. Then she said, "I'm not sure he's come home yet, Mrs Grout, but let me check, and I'll call you right back. All right? Well, I appreciate your concern."

She hung up. "They want to come over. To 'talk over the wonderful event'."

"I'll bet," said Billy's father. "With six lawyers. Now let's think this out before we do anything. It's important."

He sighed and glanced at Billy. "Right?"

Billy nodded miserably.

"Well, it's better than nothing," said his father, taking the scraps of paper. "Except there's nothing to prove when you wrote them. Why are they both torn off the pad?"

"But it shows that he wasn't going to use Tom's numbers if he didn't even bother to write them all down." said Billy's mother.

"Think about it," said his father. "Billy, why are they just scraps of paper?"

Billy had torn off everything around the

two discarded sets of numbers because that was where he'd decoded the words he'd gotten from Janie. "I just, you know – it was just whatever paper was around."

"John, do you really think we should even talk to them before we call Larry?" said his mother.

"We're not going to talk," said his father. "We're going to listen. When you get into something like this, you want to find out as much about the other side as you can, and people are a lot more likely to let something slip if they think it's just a friendly conversation, before anyone's even mentioned the word lawyer."

The doorbell rang.

"OK, Helen, you show them into the living room. Billy, you come with me. I want you to tell me who everyone is."

"Tom and his parents, Mr and Mrs Grout. You've met them before," whispered Billy, peeking around the swinging door from the kitchen.

"And Alan and his mother. Why would—"

"Shh," said his father. "Just tell me who they are."

"Joe and his father? And Frankie and Joe's sister!"

"You mean the boy who bought the ticket for you?"

"Joe's sister is his girlfriend. That must be all. Mum's shutting the door."

"Okay, you go sit on the back steps." His father pushed past him through the swinging door.

PUNCTURE WOUNDS!
PUNCTURE WOUNDS!

Billy sat down on the bottom step. After a while Joe and Alan and Tom came out the kitchen door. Tom came down the steps past Billy and went across the driveway and sat down on the kerb. He didn't look at Billy.

Alan said, "Hi, Billy," and went over and said something to Tom and then came back and sat on the kerb about halfway between them.

Joe walked back and forth on the top step. Like Admiral Napoleon on the poop deck, thought Billy. After a while Joe began to snort scornfully. Then he said, "Boy, my father is going to eat your parents up. Ground meat! Chopped radishes! Boy."

Nobody said anything.

"I mean, you talk about MASSACRES!" crowed Joe. "I mean blood on the floor and gore all over the ceiling, eyeballs stuck to the walls. People withered with insults down to like the size of itty-bitty dried wrinkled peas of dog poo. Boy."

"Yeah, and you're so big," said Billy. "You won the lottery. You've got so much money you don't know how to spend it. You're not even in this."

"Witnesses get paid!" said Joe. "Witnesses get paid!"

"Yeah, if they lie!" yelled Billy, jumping up and charging into him. They fell grappling on the top step.

"Watch out! We'll fall off the steps! Come on!" Joe managed to break away as Billy rolled off the top step. The cellarway clanged under him. Joe scrabbled around so his back was to the door. "Stay back! I got my brother's spikes on!" He was kicking and thrashing his arms around so Billy couldn't jump him again. "You'll get puncture wounds! Puncture wounds!"

But Billy was brushing himself off. "You're just like my little sister. Whenever anyone touches her, she falls down on her back and kicks and waves her arms like a bug."

Joe stopped kicking.

"You haven't got spikes on," said Tom.

"He's got his sister's spikes on," said Billy. "Girls' spikes have pretend ones because they don't want to hurt anyone."

Joe squinted at him, thinking. Then he suddenly dabbed at his cheek with his hand and looked at his fingers. "Blood! Geez, sissy Billy's scratching again."

"You scratched yourself waving your hands all around." Billy imitated him girlishly. "Oo oo, prease don't hurd me. Puffer wounds! Puffer wounds!"

"Shh!" said Alan suddenly.

The muffled sounds of people yelling could be heard from inside the house.

"It's them!"

"Quick." Billy heaved up the cellar door and laid it carefully back. "We can probably hear them from the cellar. Shh."

They tiptoed single file down into the cellar.

MARTIAN REAL ESTATE

"Be my guest!" Billy's father was almost yelling. "Be my guest!"

"John," Billy's mother was saying. "John. John."

"You think the word lawyer scares us?" It was Tom's mother. "Only people who are lying and cheating and stealing—"

But then the rumbling that had been running under the other voices like a subway train burst out, and Joe's father was drowning the rest out.

"Ap Bac, Binh Gia, Dong Xoai. You think I haven't seen some spectacular displays of firepower? I was in Nam. Everybody yelling and screaming. You think you're going to scare me? You think I care what kinds of names you and your lawyers call me? When we came back from Nam, the peaceniks and hippies waved flags in our faces; everybody else was too busy counting their profits, the politicians and lawyers sucking up money out of both sides of their mouths. Linda! Frankie!"

The front door slammed.

A few moments later it slammed again.

"That was probably my parents," whispered Tom.

"Come on," whispered Billy. "We don't want them to know we've been listening."

They tiptoed back toward the cellarway.

"Where's Joe?"

"He must have gone."

"No," said Alan. "He's there." He pointed into the dimness by the old coal bin.

Joe was just standing there, half-silhouetted against one of the little windows. They couldn't see his face.

"Joe? We're going."

"What are you doing?" asked Tom.

"He's scared of his father," said Alan. "I've seen him before when his father yells."

"He was just boasting about him," said Billy.

It was almost as if Joe could have changed into a werewolf or something, just standing there in the dimness. But it was only because they couldn't see his face. Billy reached up, groping in the air for the string dangling from the cellar light, but before he could find it, Joe charged out of the dimness, knocking Alan into Billy and Tom, and disappeared up the steps of the cellarway.

"He was crying," said Tom.

"My mother says his father beat up a man who works for him so bad once, he had to go to the hospital," said Alan. "She says it's because his parents were awful to him. And then he was a marine in Vietnam, too."

They went up out of the cellar. Billy lowered the door shut behind them. Everything outside looked different at first. Like after an exciting movie. But then they remembered about Billy winning the lottery, their parents fighting.

"Well, I gotta go," said Tom.

"Yeah," said Alan.

Billy watched them go off. But they weren't walking together; Alan was obviously lagging behind on purpose.

"Billy, come up here." His father was standing in the kitchen door watching Alan and Tom. Billy wondered for an instant if he should just run and never come back. "Billy, I said come up here."

Billy slid past his father into the kitchen. He could see how Joe could be afraid of his father. Like now, when Dad was so angry he wouldn't even look at him.

"Oh no, we're just going to listen," said his mother. "We're not going to say anything. If people even hear the word lawyer, they get uptight."

"All right then!" yelled his father. "You handle it! I wash my hands of the whole thing! You know so much, you handle it!"

"Oh. Certainly. Now that you've got everything embroiled, now that everyone's just shouting."

"You think it would have done any good? They'd all decided already their kid had won the lottery, not Billy. Oh, they'll give us a share. It was Billy's idea originally; he's holding the winning ticket."

"But did it do any good to lose your temper? To begin yelling and screaming like them?"

Billy started to push open the door to the hall.

"Where are you going?"

"I have to go to the bathroom." There wasn't any point in standing around while they were arguing. Billy waited. Nobody said anything. He said again. "I have to go to the bathroom."

"All right. Go on."

As the door swung shut behind him, Billy heard his father sit down hard at the table.

"Look. The only thing we can do is call Larry first thing tomorrow morning."

"You have his home phone. Don't you think it's important enough to call today? That man must be crazy—"

FIGHTING CROCODILES

Billy couldn't get anything straight. Everything was all messed up. He'd won, and now everybody was trying to... Except he'd sort of won it with Janie's numbers. Except he hadn't. They hadn't been numbers, just sounds, not even really words; he'd had to figure out how to decode them into numbers. Besides, Janie could have asked Mum or Dad to buy her a lottery ticket, but she was too young to even know what she was really doing; she'd just been playing lottery. If you took the goal differences of the top four teams in the Premiership and won the lottery, it didn't mean you had to split with Wayne Rooney or Frank Lampard and the others if you won. Or like if you took how many bombs were dropped in World War II... Billy wondered what had happened to Joe's father in Vietnam.

He heard a rattle of pebbles against the window beside his bed.

Billy sat up, then slid out of bed. It was Joe, motioning to him to come down.

"Hi, Billy."

"Hey, Billy-o, come on in."

Linda's and Frankie's voices came from the dark pup tent, silvery in the moonlight. Billy looked in. Joe was holding the flap open. "Go on in."

But it was so dark inside the tent, he couldn't see where Frankie and Linda were; he didn't want to crawl right in on top of them. He felt gingerly ahead of him. Suppose Mr O'Hara was in there too and suddenly the tent would light up and Mr O'Hara would be crouching over him with a huge bloody combat knife? Billy's fingers touched a knee.

"Oh Billy," squeaked Frankie. "I didn't know you cared."

Joe was shoving in behind him. "Push in."

A match flared, revealing a confusion of faces, feet, arms, knees, heads crammed around a stub of candle stuck in the dirt.

"Don't!" said Joe into Billy's ear. "Dad'll see it."

"One little candle," whispered Frankie, holding the match to the wick, his arm reaching around under Linda's leg.
"Anyway, he's asleep."

"No!" Linda's hand slid
under Billy's chin and
pushed the candle over.
The match went out.
"He gets up all the time.
His nightmares."

"You always say he fakes them," hissed Joe.

"That doesn't mean he doesn't get up."

"What – what does he have nightmares about?" asked Billy into the darkness.

"The war dances of the Viet Cong," said Frankie.

He and Linda laughed.

"Yeah, except if he knew we were here, it'd be for real," said Joe.

In the sudden silence Billy could hear everyone breathing. But they were crammed so close together, he couldn't even tell how many people were in the tent. It sounded like about forty.

"Yeah. OK," whispered Frankie finally. "See, Billy, that's why we got Joe to get you. Mr O'Hara's – he's—"

"He's crazy," whispered Linda. Now her voice seemed to be coming from the other side of Billy. "He almost looked like he was going to punch Frankie when Frankie said he was going to buy a car for us, for after we're married. With our share."

"He wants to invest all our shares in his business," said Joe. "Buy new trucks and stuff."

"What he doesn't spend on lawyers," said Frankie, "fighting because your father got him so mad."

"So see, in two weeks when I'm eighteen, I'm going to run away and marry Frankie," said Linda, "and we're going to tell my father it's none of his business; he doesn't have anything to do with it because we've already made an agreement, you and me and Frankie. There's not going to be a big fight, with lawyers and all, about anything."

"More money for us," said Joe.

Billy could feel his spit right in his face.

"So here's what we figured would be fair," said Frankie. "Now, see—" And he launched into a long explanation of how the money was to be divided up.

Listening in the darkness – now and then someone scratched his leg, thinking it was their own, or Linda, probably, knocked her head against his when she pushed her hair back, sweat trickling down his face, his back and legs hurting because he couldn't straighten up – he was afraid he'd touch Linda somewhere – Billy realised they could beat him up. Three against one. Because they were crazy, acting like they'd won the lottery as much as him. He'd seen Linda get Joe down and sit on him once; she'd even bit him when he wouldn't stop squirming; his cheek and arm had been all scratched.

"So, see, the lottery commission divides the payments up, so much a year; so since you and Joe won't need the big money now—"

"As much as us," whispered Linda, "because we're getting married."

She squeezed Billy's leg and snuggled her cheek against the top of his head, so he

thought at first she was
showing him how easily
she could take him down
if he wouldn't agree with
them. But then he realised
she thought he was Frankie;
it was love. He pulled away.

"Frankie, what's the matter? Don't you love me any more?"

A hand groped at Billy's neck.

Billy ducked out from under, pushing back. The side flap of the tent was loose behind him.

"Frank always loves you," whispered Frankie.

"Hey, come on!" said Joe. "Who's trying to kiss me?"

Billy squirmed slowly, gingerly, backward, his chin on his knees, out under the side flap, pushing and pulling with his hands.

"Will you come on!" said Joe out loud. "I'll tell Mum you were poking me!"

"I wouldn't poke you with a ten–foot pole, nerd," said Linda.

"Shh," hissed Frankie.

Billy stood up quietly outside the tent. Then he turned and started silently away.

"You pinched me!" hissed Joe.

"I didn't. Just get your arm off my hair."

"I'm not touching your hair."

"SHH!" hissed Frankie. "Come on! Remember the money. Here, I'll get between you. OK. Now so what we decided, Billy, is you get £185,000 because it was your idea and your number, and Joe gets £50,000 because he can testify it was just your number, and Tom didn't have anything to do with it. And I—"

"We," whispered Linda.

"We," whispered Frankie, "get £175,000 because I—"

"We," whispered Linda.

"We bought the winning ticket. OK?"

But Billy was already fifteen feet away, tiptoeing across the lawn, so there was no answer.

"OK? Billy? What's the matter? That's fair. We're giving you £10,000 more than anyone else. If we don't say we bought the ticket, they'll say it's no good and nobody will – wait! Count feet! I think he's escaped!"

In the moonlight Billy could see the tent convulse. Confused voices, accusing, shushing.

"I've got him!" "That's me!" "Shh!" "Who? Him?" "No, me." "Who's me?" "I'm me; who are you?"

The tent collapsed as if six crocodiles were fighting under it. Billy fled.

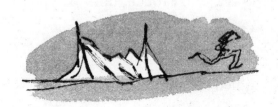

A DARK MESS

Billy pressed pause on the £199.99 DVD player.

"Don't touch, little boy," said the salesgirl, coming round the corner of the aisle.

> "Look, don't touch, until you buy
> Or I will poop you in the eye."

She giggled back delighted at the salesboy who was coming behind her pushing a cart with other DVD players on it.

Billy wanted to say, I won the lottery, zit queen, so eat your own toe lint. But Dad had said he wasn't to say anything to anybody about it, even if they asked him, even if they tortured him. He watched them arrange the other DVD players on the shelf, attaching one to the £1,695.95 Deluxe Home Entertainment Theatre. He'd have one like that in his room. There'd be another one downstairs for Mum and Dad and Janie; the walls would be all soundproofed, so if he wanted to crank it up like Donnie Winslow's older brother when their parents weren't home...

A blurry voice said above him. "You're not going to get that. You're not going to get anything."

For an instant Billy thought it was his conscience, like an angel, because of Janie's numb... But then he looked up and saw Frankenstein's monster's evil face frowning down at him from between two TVs and knew it was Alan. He'd climbed up on the display shelf in the other aisle.

"You won't," said Alan when he saw that

Billy had recognised him. "My father—"

"What are you doing? Climbing on the—"

Frankenstein's monster disappeared as the salesboy almost knocked Billy over to get round the rack at Alan. Before Billy could run, the salesgirl grabbed him by the back of his pants, almost pulling them off.

*

"My son had nothing to do with it," said Billy's mother. Billy couldn't see her because the store manager had made him stand beside him behind the high Returns counter while he called her on the public address system. "Billy isn't even a friend of those boys any more."

Billy didn't bother to tell her it had been Alan, not Tom and Joe.

"All right, lady, just get him out of the store.

My God, these kids."

"But he didn't do anything. And you know my name; you don't have to call me 'lady' as if I were some lower form of person who can be referred to generically like a sheep. I suppose that's why you built this counter so high, to put everyone else below you."

Staring into the dark messy shelf in front of him, Billy felt that that was what life was, a dark messy shelf of grown-up junk. He felt a hand plop down on his head. It steered him silently through the half-door back out to where Janie and Mum were waiting.

*

"Billy," said Janie, tears trembling in her voice, tugging at his sleeve. "Billy, those trousers talked to me."

"Trousers can't talk." Billy was pretending he'd be able to

buy any football shirt he wanted, when everything was settled. But he knew it wouldn't make any difference; he'd still be scared he was going to get hit in the face by the ball.

"Billy, they did," said Janie. "Do trousers have teeth?"

"The zips do," said Billy. "Don't get too close to the zips."

"Billy! Mummy!"

"Shh. You'll get us kicked out of the store."

"Then protect me from the zips." Janie clung to him. "See, they're all around, hanging from the racks like snooks."

"Snakes," said Billy. "You're not really scared."

"I am. The trousers really did speak to me."

The sign above the circular rack read: Tracksuit bottoms £10.99!

"What'd they say?" Billy stepped back. Yeah, now he could see Alan's feet and legs under the dangling tracksuits.

"I don't know."

Billy looked round for something to poke Alan's feet with. But then he realised, what was the point? Alan would make a fuss, Mum would get mad; it was stupid, just like everything else. He'd won the lottery, he'd won the lottery... And what difference had it made? Everything was worse. Now he didn't even have the fun of pretending what it would be like if he won; he didn't have the fun of figuring out the numbers; he didn't have any friends; he had to hang around in department stores with Mum and Janie. Not that he wanted friends who only thought about money, who only thought about cheating him out of the money he'd won, the money they hadn't had anything to do with...

The monster was glaring at him from among the tracksuit bottoms. "Tom's parents told my parents I should get a reward if I can remember that even some of the numbers Tom

told you were the winning ones. They want me and Tom to be hypnotised so we'll remember better. My parents are finding out what hypnosis does to you. My mother says I'm weird enough as it is because I even want to wear this Frankenstein monster mask during meals."

"It's so scary outside it," said Janie. "It must be twice as scary inside. So why do you?"

"People can't call me Moony and Four Eyes because of my glasses," said Alan. "But mostly because then no one can tell what I'm thinking, especially my mother and father."

"Janie? Billy?" Their mother came round the rack. "Oh hello, Alan."

"I'm not supposed to talk to you," said Alan.

"If you were really Frankenpoop, it wouldn't matter," said Janie.

"You mean because of the lottery?" said Billy's mother.

The Frankenstein monster mask nodded.

"Unfortunately, your parents are probably right. But we'll hope that all that will be over soon and things can go back to normal. Come, Janie, Billy."

"Suppose it sticks to his face and he can't get it off so he really turns into Frankenstone?" said Janie, running after her.

"He's too stupid!!" said Billy. And he pushed Alan so hard he fell down backward through the tracksuit bottoms.

"Hey—"

Billy followed his mother and Janie across the parking lot. He shouldn't have just pushed Alan; he should have stomped his face! He was just like the others, trying to cheat him out of his money!

BLURRED BLACK
BUG'S BLOOD

"You're lying to me, Billy! Look at me! No, don't look at your father! Look at me, damn it." Mr Enright grabbed Billy's chin and held it so he couldn't turn his head. "You didn't just 'think up' those numbers. You got them from somewhere. Just like you got your other numbers. You've told me how you got them, how you figured and figured. Billy, look at me. NOW...TELL...ME...HOW...YOU...GOT... THE...NUMBERS...THAT...WON."

"Larry, take it easy," said Billy's father. "He's just a boy."

"Think, Billy," said Mr Enright, not letting go of his chin or taking his eyes off him.

"Think." Without turning his head, he said to Billy's father, "If we have to put him on the stand, they're going to be a lot rougher than I'm being."

Billy burst into tears, wrenching his chin out of Mr Enright's fingers, hiding his face on his knees.

"That's not going to help you on the stand," said Mr Enright. "Judges don't let crybabies off."

"I – I got them from – from Janie," sobbed Billy.

"From Janie? Who's Janie?"

"His little sister."

"Billy, Billy," said Mr Enright, mussing Billy's hair. He laughed. "I almost dropped my load when you dragged in another person, and a woman at that. But it's perfect. You've just blown that one kid out of the water. You're sure you've got those scraps of paper you transposed Janie's words on?"

Sniffing. Billy nodded.

"We'll make a lawyer of him," said Mr Enright to Billy's father. "Meticulous, saves everything. Billy, you get a reward before we go on." He pressed the buzzer on his desk.

His secretary came in. "Mrs Scurry, an ice-cream cone. Billy, what flavour?"

"Chocolate."

"With sprinkles?"

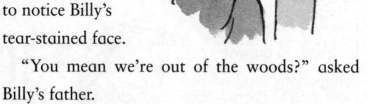

Billy nodded. Mrs Scurry went out. She hadn't even seemed to notice Billy's tear-stained face.

"You mean we're out of the woods?" asked Billy's father.

Mr Enright snorted. "We're out of one wood. Ready to plunge into another. There may be ten woods, twenty, before we're through. Remember the other side – or sides – are somewhere out there right now doing just what we're doing, trying to figure out how to win."

"By hook or by crook."

"Probably. Maybe, if we're lucky, only by hook, not crook, though all's fair with love and war and huge sums of money."

"Maybe we should try to settle it."

"Not now. They'd just see it as weakness. Besides, do you really want to give them something if they don't deserve it? I'm not saying yet they don't, but just assuming that's what we come to, that the money should be all yours."

"But if it's going to be messy. You said it could take a couple of years."

"The money's not going to go anywhere. It'll be in a special account, earning interest. And as far as I can see from my conversations with the Grout and O'Hara lawyers, it's going to be messy whatever we do; messy and nasty."

"All right." Billy's father sighed and sat down. "Go ahead."

Mr Enright turned back to Billy. "OK, now Billy, sit up straight, hands together in your lap. Any rehearsal we can get for the witness stand, we have to take, because it may really be rough on you up there. They'll badger you, try to mix you up, make you forget, bang bang bang bang—" He broke off and turned back to Billy's father. "John, there's something you and Helen should think carefully about. I don't think Janie really has a competing claim here, and in any case since both kids are minors, you and Helen have a lot of latitude to interpret what's right for both. But I know in recent years Helen has become interested in women's issues, and so I want you two to thrash the whole thing out before we get to court. A trial can be a real b—" He glanced at Billy. "—glitch for everyone, and we don't want something like how the money's to be divided, if it is, between Billy and Janie to come up, to be brought up by one of the other parties – as a diversion, to confuse, whatever. You have to realise—"

Billy had stopped really trying to understand everything his father and Mr Enright said almost as soon as he and Dad had got to Mr Enright's office. Of course, he understood what Mr Enright was asking him, and he was trying to remember everything that had happened and all, but it was like everything was blurred; he almost felt dizzy; even familiar things seemed strange. He'd always thought Mrs Grout, Tom's mother, was nice and all, but that's not the way Mr Enright and dad and even Mum last night talked about her. They talked about her almost as if she was crazy. Joe and Linda had talked about their father like that. It was like the whole world had changed; suddenly maybe there could be a real Frankenstein's monster – like when you thought about what World War III would really be like, when you weren't just playing *Star Wars* or World of Warcraft in somebody's attic.

BOTTOM

He heard the cellar door open, the first step creak.

"Billy?" called his mother. "What are you doing down there?"

"Nothing."

More creaks. Now she was probably leaning down so she could see him. In a minute she'd say it wasn't healthy to spend so much time in a damp dark cellar.

More creaks. She was coming all the way down. He didn't look around or even bother to get down off the box he was standing on to look out the little window.

"You've been down here for two hours," she

said. A final creak. She'd probably sat down on the bottom step. "Have you been looking out the window? When I was your age, I used to like to go down into our cellar and look at the street through the little windows. Everything looked different, new. Even a little exciting. I saw things I hadn't noticed before. I'd never paid any attention to people's shoes, for instance. I used to try to guess what kind of people they were from their shoes." She paused. "It also works from attic windows, except this house doesn't have an attic. Then you see people from above. I always hoped I'd see a robber with stolen jewels hidden in a hole he'd made on top of his – or her – hair by working up the hair around the sides. And then I'd be a hero and get a reward."

Billy didn't say anything. Things had looked kind of new and interesting out the little window at first. And he'd also noticed how the space right outside the window, between the window and the flower bed, was like a secret little country with ants and bugs for people, stones and pale weeds for tall buildings.

After a while his mother said, "I guess it's pretty disappointing, winning the lottery and all it means is this mess."

Billy shrugged.

"But you know even if there hadn't been all this—"

Now she was going to give her speech about how disappointments were inevitable, and then she'd drag in how life was like going down a river in a boat: sometimes it was smooth, the sun was shining, the banks were full of trees with happy animals among them, elephants and monkeys and herons. But sometimes on both banks there were just ugly abandoned factories and burned houses; you saw dead rats floating beside the boat. Whenever anything happened, even something good, she always made the same speech.

"We would have had to put most of the money away for your college; the toys you would have bought – because, of course, we wouldn't have put away all the money – you would have got tired of—"

She didn't even know he didn't buy toys any more. She was always saying, "Your trail bike isn't a toy. Remember that, Billy."

"You can't buy happiness with money."

He almost said, I could buy you. And then throw you out on the junkheap.

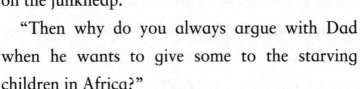

"Then why do you always argue with Dad when he wants to give some to the starving children in Africa?"

"I don't always. And I'm not saying money isn't important. Of course, it's much worse not to have any. Or enough."

"Enough for what?"

"Enough for what we need, like food and electricity."

"You're always saying. 'Oh, John, if we just didn't have to worry about the mortgage every month, if we just had enough not to worry.'"

"Well, sometimes everyone worries, but I know as long as you and Janie and Daddy are all right—"

Now she was going to make her speech about mush! She didn't know anything! All she ever did was make speeches!

"I have to go." He tried to jump onto the stairs behind the step she was sitting on but his foot slipped. She caught him and had a chance to hug him, even start to say, "Poor Bil—" before he could break free and escape up the stairs.

STARTING OVER

Billy climbed over the stone wall behind the cemetery and wandered up along the trail bike ruts through Magaden's field, not paying any attention to his feet stumbling in the dried mud of the ruts because that's what everything was, stupid, a mess, so what difference did it make? At the top of the rise he stopped. At the bottom of the next field was Marsh's Swamp. When he'd been little, he'd been scared to go into it because he'd thought there was quicksand and copperheads and even trolls. The trolls lived under the scummy stagnant water; they made the bubbles you could see sometimes rising to the surface, glittering oilily in the sunshine and then bursting. But then two years ago he and Joe and

Tom had made an expedition – geez, even two years ago they'd been so stupid. They'd all got long poles and sharpened the ends, supposedly to pull each other out of the mud but really for stabbing anything that tried to come out of the pools at them, not that he'd believed it even then. And the whole thing had turned out to be nothing; they'd just got all muddy and bitten by bugs and had come out on Cedar Street among the rubbish bins behind the launderette.

Something white flashed among the trees just inside the swamp.

It was too big for just a pigeon or something.

It was probably just an old rag somebody had thrown into the woods after cleaning their trail bike. Even in the middle of the swamp he and Joe and Tom had come on an old rusted Volkswagen bug up to its doors in a pool.

It was moving, so it couldn't be a rag. Maybe it was like a wounded rare egret, and he'd catch it and nurse it back to health and get a reward, and there'd be like this big ceremony when they let it go, everybody watching it circling higher and higher and higher...

It didn't move like a bird. A bird wouldn't be running and then stopping and then running, like it was trying to catch things among the trees. Billy ran crouching down the hill, heading away from the direction the white thing seemed to be going. Clambering over the wall, he ran from tree to tree. And then, just as he reached the edge of a clearing, he saw the white thing flash among the trees on the other side of the clearing – it was coming toward him.

And Amy Miller, in white shorts, blouse, sneakers, high socks, a pith helmet! – with a butterfly net! – came out of the trees jumping from one hummock of marsh grass to the next. She made a lunge at what Billy saw now was a tiny yellow butterfly, missed, almost fell. But the swamp was so dry, there were hardly any mud-holes. And then, lunging again, she caught the butterfly. She knelt on a hummock and carefully opened a box she had on her belt and took out a little bottle. Then she took off the pith helmet and wiped her forehead on her sleeve. She was all muddy and sweaty. She wasn't crazy; she was catching butterflies.

Billy started out from behind the tree and then stopped and waited to see if anyone was with her. They hadn't really said anything at all to each other since the dumb stuff with Joe and his sister Rena and the others. Of course, they'd seen each other in school. Once she'd been at Rena and Joe's house when he and Alan had gone to find Joe. They'd both acted like nothing had really happened, and of course it hadn't really. When he'd lifted her big floppy hat and sort of kissed her, it hadn't been anything but an experiment, like trying to put four candy bars into your mouth at one time. That was probably why she'd never said anything about it to anyone, just like he hadn't.

Billy stepped out from behind the tree and pretended to cough.

"Why are you catching butterflies?"

The frightened look on her face turned to deliberate indifference.

"It's my collection, so I'll have it when I go to college, to study."

"I thought you were going to be an actress."

"I am, but it's hard to make money in acting, so you have to have some other way to earn it when you're starting out."

He could see the butterfly still moving in the net. "It's still alive."

"I have to kill it."

He watched her open the little bottle and

carefully take the butterfly
out of the net and put it in
the bottle. In an instant the
butterfly was dead.

Or at least it'd stopped moving.

"Is it dead? Can I touch it?"

"Just with this pick. Lightly on its body. This part. You might hurt its wings."

Billy touched the butterfly with the tip of the pick. He couldn't feel anything. It didn't look any different. Except, of course, it was so still.

"See, that little thing's its maxilla. And its eyes and its antenna, its palp, its thorax." Amy pointed to the parts of the butterfly. Her hair brushed Billy's cheek. He pushed it away.

"What's the matter?"

"I thought it was a mosquito."

"Lots of people collect butterflies," said Amy. "There's even a club in secondary school."

"How about bugs?" said Billy. "Like those big beetles with pinchers." He curved out his arms. "Hofe hofe. Or like June beetles, which are about four inches long."

"Miss Simons collects caterpillars," said Amy. "She's the one who's helping me with my collection, so she could probably help you with beetles. That could be your first one."

She pointed to a beetle clambering in a hummock of marsh grass.

"Yeah," said Billy. But he didn't know how you caught beetles. Beetles weren't like butterflies; beetles could probably bite you. Amy glanced at him and then deftly reached out and plucked the beetle out of the grass and taking the cork out of her little bottle with the heel of the same hand, popped the beetle in, corked the bottle and held it up. "See?"

The beetle started to scrabble its legs against the glass and then stopped. One leg pawed feebly – the beetle was still.

"Yuck," said Billy, grinning.

"Miss Simons says you kill anything you collect unless you study it. Then you bring it back to life."

"Not people."

"People are different."

"How about money?"

"You mean because you won the lottery even though you might not get the money?"

"My dad's lawyer says we will."

"Rena says her sister and Frankie know they're trying to cheat you."

"My mother and father are going to make me put most of it away for college anyway."

"That's what mine said they'd do too. So, see you'll have this big collection of like dead money."

"But boy, when I get to be eighteen, they can't make me spend it on college. I could buy like a Ferrari, Vadoom doom." He pretended he was shifting gears, easing into the lap turn at the Grand Prix.

"But you'd still have to have something to do," said Amy. "If all you are is rich, it's stupid. I mean, do people treat you any different now than before you won? You're still just who you were before but with like this big golden tent growing up out of your head and covering you so no one can even see you any more. All they see and shake hands with and...and..." Amy couldn't remember everything her mother had said; she hadn't been paying that much attention; it'd just been another of her mother's speeches – "is the tent, not you. Underneath you're still the same. Except under the tent it's hot and stuffy, and it's hard to walk, and there's lots of places you can't even go, like over to other people's houses, because you can't get through the doors and you take up so much room."

Amy had got up and was clumping around among the hummocks with her cheeks puffed out and her eyes crossed and her arms curved out like a gorilla's. Geez, she was the craziest girl; she wasn't like a girl; she was more like a boy. Only since she wasn't a boy, it was different.

"And everybody's trying to cheat you," said Billy.

"It's dead," said Amy.

She had stopped clumping and was looking at the little glass bottle. They dumped the beetle out into a tiny specimen box Amy had, and she showed him how to label it – number 1, because it was his first specimen – and the date and where it had been caught and all, and then she said he could have half of her sandwich. They sat on hummocks talking and eating. She also told him that if you really worked at it and made this terrific collection, you could sell it, which is what she might have to do because it was so hard to get into theatre or movies or TV. Sometimes you had to take awful parts like on soap operas. Billy noticed how she had this way of licking the perspiration off her upper lip with the tip of her tongue. Her knees shone in the sun. He told her how he'd figured out the numbers from Janie's nonsense words. And then they caught a butterfly which Billy noticed fluttering along by the woods on the other side of the clearing, and a beetle they both almost stepped on capturing the butterfly. Every time Billy remembered the lottery mess, it seemed further and further away – as if it were on Mars, and where they were, even though there were mosquitoes (but Amy had repellent), was the only real thing.

Except, of course, he knew it wasn't. You couldn't live in a swamp. So then for a moment he felt dizzy, almost like he did when he was afraid he was going to be carsick, especially if he was with someone else's parents. But then, when they got to the wall at the edge of the swamp, Amy turned around and said she was going over to Miss Simons's tomorrow, and if he wanted, she'd call and ask if he could come too. So then Billy forgot about the other stuff again, like Mr Enright and Mr O'Hara yelling at him, and concentrated on going to Miss Simons's.

EPILOGUE

But a week later it was suddenly settled: Tom got £5,000, Frankie (and Linda) got £20,000, Alan got £1,000, Joe (or really his father) got £2,500. And Billy? Billy got £381,500. He explained it to Amy and Miss Simons: he had the winning ticket, the actual tiny piece of paper, and it didn't, of course, have anybody's name on it, so his father could have turned it in, even if Billy couldn't have because he wasn't old enough to play the lottery. But then Frankie (and Linda) could have sued because even though there had been a written contract between Frankie and Billy, there was all sorts of legal junk: minors like Billy weren't supposed to make contracts; but people who were old enough, like Frankie, weren't supposed to make contracts with minors. So what would a judge do? Give the money to Frankie, who'd done something he shouldn't have and even taken Billy's money to do it and then decided he was going to keep all the profits for himself? Or Billy? But Billy had also done something he shouldn't, even if it was dumb to say kids couldn't play the lottery. And there was a lot more to it. Even Billy's father hadn't really understood it all. But anyway it was this huge mess that would have taken years to straighten out – it could have gone to the Supreme Court. And then finally the lottery commission might have decided nobody should get the money.

"But you said you didn't use Tom's numbers," said Amy. "So why should he get anything? And Joe didn't have anything to do with it."

"Well, see, when you settle something, you're supposed to try to give everybody something just so they can't bring it all up again later," said Billy. "Like if Joe hadn't got anything, his father might have sued just because he was mad. My mother says Joe's father has always been like that. When they were in high school, he was always fighting – even his own teammates on the football team."

"Well." Amy looked doubtful.

"Three hundred and eighty-one thousand, five hundred pounds," said Miss Simons dreamily, holding the beetle she'd just tweezered up out of a specimen jar. She put the beetle on the milk-glass dissecting board. "What are you going to do with it all?"

"Well, I only get about two hundred and twenty-nine thousand because of taxes," said Billy, trying to be serious. But then he couldn't help grinning. "But my parents are putting most of it away for when I go to college."

"How much are you going to get now?" asked Amy.

"They haven't decided."

His father had really said maybe Billy wasn't going to get anything now; he certainly wasn't until he showed he understood that he couldn't just do as he pleased, that if he wasn't supposed to play the lottery until he was eighteen or keep on with a bet or anything, then he wasn't to do it. It didn't matter if it was fun or clever or funny or his friends all wanted him to, he wasn't to do it.

"Have you made things up with your friends?" said Miss Simons.

"No." Billy shook his head.

"They're creeps," said Amy. "They lied and everything."

But when Billy got home, Tom and Joe and Alan were waiting for him on the front porch steps.

"We've come for our shares," said Joe. But he was grinning.

Billy just looked at them: if his mother was home, it'd be all right. Otherwise they'd catch him while he was trying to get his key into the lock of the kitchen door – three against one.

"My parents gave me ten dollars," said Tom "How much did you get?"

"They haven't decided."

"You'd think it was our parents who won the lottery," said Alan. "If I hadn't told mine, they wouldn't even know about it now."

"How much did your father give you?" Billy asked Joe.

"Five pounds," said Joe. "I just put it in my mouth and chewed till finally he asked me what I was doing. So I said, 'You really want to see? Bend down and look.' Go on," Joe said to Alan, "look."

Joe opened his mouth, and Alan bent down.

Joe spat a whole wad of something right into his face.

"Come on! Geez." Alan wiped his face. "Your father would have... You wouldn't be here now."

He went over to the tap on the side of the house to wash his face.

"Yeah?" said Joe, picking up the wad and smoothing it out on his knee. It was a five-pound note.

"I bet you didn't even think of that till now," said Tom.

"You think I care about five pounds?" said Joe. He held up the wet, wrinkled note and tore it neatly in half and let the two halves flutter to the pavement.

But Billy noticed he was watching Tom, who was closest, to make sure he didn't try to grab them. After a minute he bent down to pick them up as if he didn't really care, but Alan suddenly glopped a whole handful of mud onto his face from behind and, snatching up one of the halves, missing the other, fled across the lawn. Joe ran after him, wiping the mud off his cheek. Alan tripped and fell, dropping the half-note. Joe stopped to pick it up. Alan vanished into the bushes beside Morgan's house. Joe plunged after him.

Tom and Billy looked at the half-note still on the pavement.

"Now we got him," said Billy.

But neither of them picked it up.

"My mother says money is the root of all evil," said Tom.

"Yeah."

"And then she spends an hour arguing with my father because roast beef is a pound more per person than turkey for my sister's wedding and he won't pay it."

"Maybe he just likes turkey better," said Billy. He wondered how much longer Tom was going to stay. He hadn't had a chance to even look at the beetles he'd caught yesterday under the old barn behind the wall.

Alan crawled out from under the porch, panting, his face and clothes streaked with sweat and mud. "I think I lost him."

"GERONIMO!" Joe hurled over the porch railing. They went down in a heap. Alan scrabbled free and took off across the lawn, Joe after him. Joe paused to pick up a stick and fling it after him like a spear. They vanished again into the bushes beside Morgan's house.

"Everybody's always fighting and making up, fighting and making up," said Tom. "I don't know why things can't just" – he shrugged – "you know, go along."

"Then it'd be boring," said Billy.

"Yeah, but then at least you wouldn't get scared."

Tom was rubbing his eyebrows; Billy couldn't see his face, so he couldn't see if there were tears in his eyes. The shadows lengthened across the lawn. Billy could hear the mourning doves cooing in the field behind the barn. After a while he said, "You should take up beetles."

"Beetles?"

"Yeah. You collect them. Come on, I'll show you."

He started up the steps but then went back down and picked up the half-bill and put it in his pocket. "If it was the other way around, Joe'd bug us."

Going up the stairs to his room, Tom clumping behind him, he decided he didn't have to tell Tom about Amy. If Tom came, it wouldn't be the same at Miss Simons's.

IF YOU LIKE HOW TO GET FABULOUSLY RICH, YOU'LL LOVE

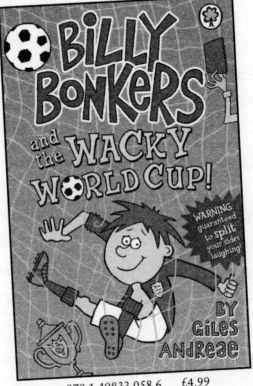

978 1 40833 058 6   £4.99

ORCHARD